3 3500 56330 2868

8.57
9/13

S0-AEI-736

First published in 2013

Copyright © Text, Lockley Lodge Pty Ltd, 2013
Copyright © Illustrations, diagrams, handmade fonts, Andrew Weldon, 2013

All rights reserved. No part of this book may be reproduced or transmitted in any
form or by any means, electronic or mechanical, including photocopying, recording
or by any information storage and retrieval system, without prior permission
in writing from the publisher. The *Australian Copyright Act 1968* (the Act) allows
a maximum of one chapter or ten per cent of this book, whichever is the greater,
to be photocopied by any educational institution for its educational purposes
provided that the educational institution (or body that administers it) has given
a remuneration notice to Copyright Agency Limited (CAL) under the *Act*.

Allen & Unwin
83 Alexander Street, Crows Nest NSW 2065, Australia
Phone: (61 2) 8425 0100
Email: info@allenandunwin.com
Web: www.allenandunwin.com

A Cataloguing-in-Publication entry is available from the
National Library of Australia: www.trove.nla.gov.au

ISBN 978 1 74331 142 4

Design by Andrew Weldon and Bruno Herfst
Set in 12 pt Dolly

This book was printed in August 2013 at McPherson's Printing Group,
76 Nelson St, Maryborough, Victoria 3465, Australia.
www.mcphersonsprinting.com.au

10 9 8 7 6 5 4 3 2 1

Paul Jennings & Andrew Weldon

DON'T LOOK NOW

BOOK FOUR

ALLEN&UNWIN
SYDNEY·MELBOURNE·AUCKLAND·LONDON

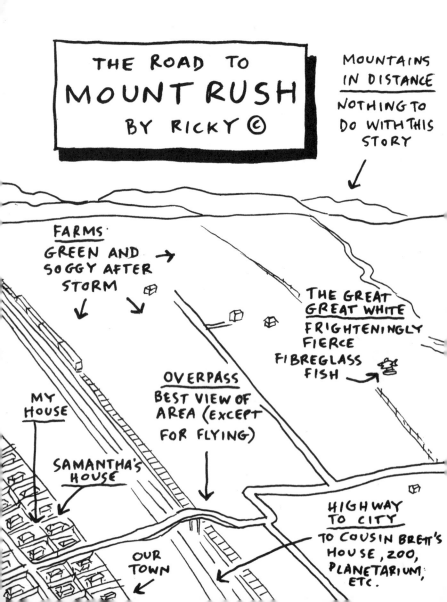

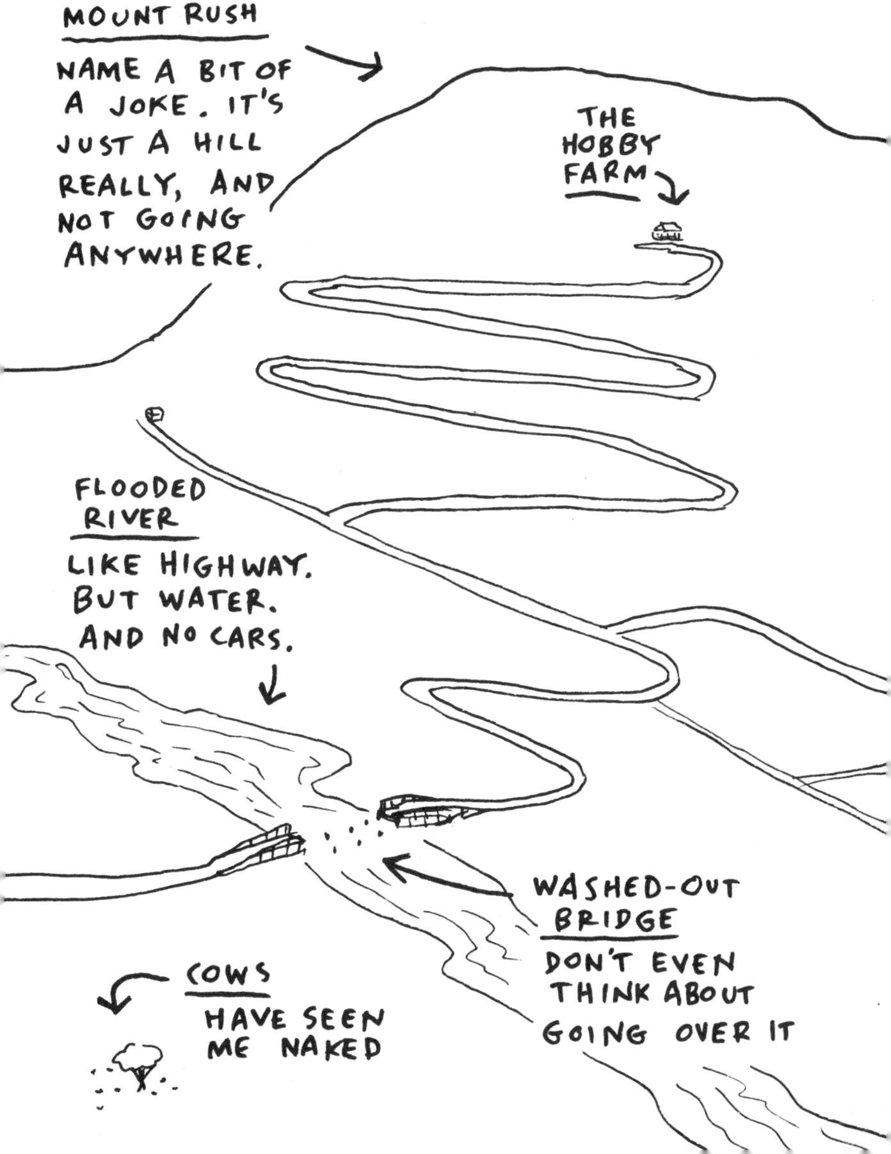
MOUNT RUSH
NAME A BIT OF A JOKE. IT'S JUST A HILL REALLY, AND NOT GOING ANYWHERE.
THE HOBBY FARM
FLOODED RIVER
LIKE HIGHWAY. BUT WATER. AND NO CARS.
WASHED-OUT BRIDGE
DON'T EVEN THINK ABOUT GOING OVER IT
COWS
HAVE SEEN ME NAKED

Story One

HOBBY FARM

1

chookhead

All was quiet in the library. We were having free reading time. Our teacher, Jenny, was moving around checking work. Some kids were on the computers, others were reading books and some were swiping and tapping their iPad screens.

I was reading my latest comic.

But I was distracted. I wanted to send a quick text to my best friend, Samantha.

Even though she was blind, she would get the message because she had a special phone for blind people.

Samantha wouldn't believe that I could fly even though I had once saved her from certain death on a cliff face.

Since then, we had become great friends. She was even nicer than I'd thought she would be.

SOME THINGS YOU SHOULD KNOW ABOUT **SAMANTHA**.

- Blind since she was born. ——

- Hardly ever takes off sunnies. —

- Very friendly and caring.
  It's embarrassing that I once
  thought she was snobby.

- Phone with clever apps for blind
  people. One lets her type messages
  in Braille, another speaks incoming
  messages out loud to her.

- Loves to listen to music. ——

- Her Guide Dog, Jack. Slobbery. —

I looked around the classroom to check that Jenny wasn't watching, then pulled out my phone. I wanted to tell Samantha why no one was allowed to see me fly. But I didn't know what to say to her.

I bit my bottom lip and thought hard. Then I tapped out a simple message.

I really can fly, but if anyone sees me
I will fall to the ground and die.

Just as I pressed the SEND button I head a loud shout. And laughter. It came from Mandy Chow. She was pointing at something.

And the something was me.

'Aah, aah, haa, haa, haa. Ricky looks like a chook.'

I felt like such a fool. I could feel my face turning red.

Jenny took the phone out of my hand and shook her head at me.

'That's enough of that,' she said to Mandy Chow.

Jenny was being kind, but I could see that she was trying not to laugh, too.

I felt stupid. I glared at Mandy Chow.

I hurried over to the sliding library door and stared sadly at my reflection.

What she said was true.

The mirror does not lie.

For the rest of the day Mandy Chow kept whispering names at me.

Finally the school day ended. Jenny gave me my phone back and I walked home. Life was terrible. Everyone in our class thought I was a fool.

Even being able to fly didn't help because I had to keep it a secret.

If people knew about my special power no one would laugh at me. I would be…

When I came home, Mum was walking down the stairs. She was carrying my doona.

More trouble.

'No,' I yelled. 'No, no, no.'

'Yes, yes, yes,' said Mum firmly. 'The time has come. This old doona is going to the tip.'

I stuck out my arms to try to stop her. She couldn't throw it out. It was covered in signs of wonderful moments from times gone by.

Happy doona-memories flooded through my mind.

THE STORY OF

MY DOONA

I grabbed one end of the doona and started tugging it back towards my bedroom.

'I love it,' I said.

'It smells of pee,' said Mum.

'Every kid wets the bed sometimes,' I said.

'I know that,' said Mum. 'But it's so stained and stinky.'

Everything was going wrong. It was a bad,
bad day.

I had to stop Mum from committing doonacide.
There was only one thing I could do. Make her
feel guilty.

'The kids at school all laughed at me,' I said.
'They said I look like a chook.'

Mum let go of the doona and I fell over backwards
onto the landing at the top of the stairs. I ran into
my room and Mum followed. We had a long talk.

She let me keep the doona.

For now.

2

The Promise

As soon as Mum left the room, my phone beeped. It was a text message from Samantha.

Come quick. Emergency. And don't pretend you can fly. :)

I knew that I could never mention flying again to Samantha. She had a thing about telling the truth. She would think I was a liar. I had to keep my mouth shut or I would be history.

An emergency. I wondered if she was stuck somewhere in the floods. It had been raining for weeks and the river was running over the highway. I ran around to her place and found her sitting on the porch with her Guide Dog, Jack.

She had her glasses off and was wiping her eyes. Her eyes were all red and weepy.

'It's The Show tomorrow,' she blurted out.

'I know,' I said. 'I'm going with Dad. To see the bulls. They've got camels too. And prizes for the best animals.'

'Everyone in my class is entering a chicken,' said Samantha. 'We could win a ribbon. Maybe even Best in Show.'

'Great,' I said.

I wasn't really into chickens, but anything to make Samantha happy.

She wiped her eyes and went on with the sad story.

'Our chickens are on the other side of the river. And the bridge is flooded. We can't get our chickens to The Show.'

Just then her mother called from inside. 'Samantha, teatime.'

Jack stood up and barked. He was hungry.

Samantha opened the door and followed Jack inside. I didn't stop to think. I did what I always did. I offered the impossible.

'I'll get your chickens for you,' I said. 'Where are they?'

'At the Hobby Farm on Mount Rush,' she answered. 'On the other side of the river. You won't be able to get across.'

As she waited at the door, I said one more stupid thing.

'Those chickens will make it to The Show.
I promise. Even if I have to fly there to fetch them.'

She didn't say a word.

She just shut the door in my face.

She would never believe that I could fly.

3

Like a Burglar

That night I snuggled down under my doona waiting for Mum and Dad to go to bed. I was worried. Very worried.

I was thinking about how I could get over the river.

I knew it would be swollen and rushing downstream. No one was allowed near it.

Carrying a couple of chooks wouldn't be too hard, but I had to do it without anyone seeing me.

And without the chickens seeing me.

If one person or animal looked at me when I was flying...

I would fall and die.

That's just the way it was.

GETTING THE CHOOKS

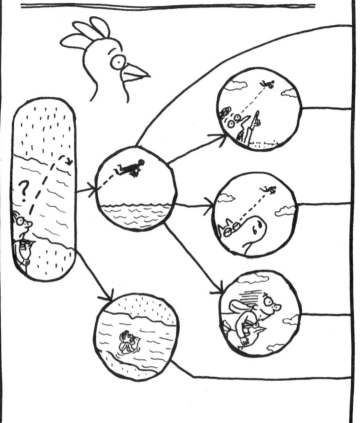

ACROSS THE RIVER

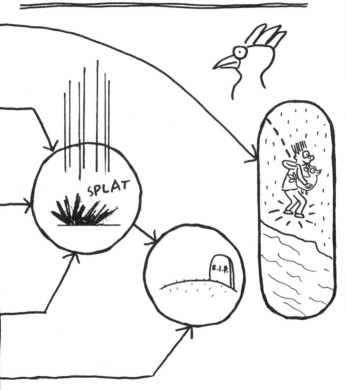

I had to get the chickens before morning. Once the first rays of sun came out, people would be out too. Rescue workers would be out on the river in boats. One of them might look up, and then I would plunge into the river and drown. And I would probably take the chickens with me.

Then Samantha would hate me. She would think I was a chicken-killer as well as a liar.

I had a sudden attack of imaginitis. Horrible thoughts entered my mind.

Perhaps they would bury the chickens with me. Me in the grave with a couple of chickens. The ancient Egyptians did that sort of thing. I wondered if the chickens would come regular or barbequed. And if fries would be included.

What if they were raw? I pushed the horrible thought out of my mind.

Mum and Dad were asleep.

It was time for action.

The night was cold, but the rain had stopped.
I felt like a burglar creeping around our backyard
in the dark.

The moon slid in and out of the clouds in silent
disapproval.

'Up,' I said to myself.

In no time at all I was flying low over the rooftops.
Then they vanished and I flew silently over
wet paddocks. And then over the swollen river.
Gurgling and rushing on its course to the sea.

I flew as quickly as I could, keeping my eyes open
for the odd owl or wallaby that might see me and
send me to my doom.

It was stupid really. Risking my life for a couple
of chooks. But I had promised Samantha. I had
to go through with it.

I knew how to get to Mount Rush, but I wasn't sure where the Hobby Farm was. It could be anywhere. Rich city people were always buying up a few acres and raising Mongolian sheep or alpacas or miniature ducks.

The city people didn't usually stay for long. They missed too many things.

Suddenly the mountain slid into view. It wasn't a mountain, really. More of a hill.

And there was only one building on it.
It had to be the place I was looking for.

I was nervous about the whole thing.

But there was no going back. I couldn't
chicken out, so I plucked up my courage
and began to descend.

I made a safe landing and quietly tiptoed up onto the verandah.

All was strangely quiet. Not a sound. Not a movement.

There they were. The chickens.

All asleep.

Silent on their perches.

Staring, staring, staring.

4

No One Stirred

There was no way I could get all those chickens across the river before morning. There were about twenty and I only had two small bin liners.

I pressed my nose against the window for a better look. The chickens stood still, like statues.

They did not move.

They did not breathe.

There was something wrong.

Oh, no. They must be dead. Their eyes were like glass.

Then I realised.

Their eyes were glass.

I stood there with my breath making fog on the glass.

The chickens stood there like stuffed toys.

They were stuffed toys.

I stepped back and looked at the sign above the entrance.

Samantha's class had made stuffed chickens to enter in the hobby section at The Show. I didn't know whether to laugh or cry.

At least I didn't have to worry about the chickens seeing me. Or pecking me. Or escaping from the bin liner as I was flying over the river.

The house was silent. The front door was unlocked. I opened it and slid inside. I bumped into something in the dark hall. Crash.

The whole world must have heard the noise.

But only I knew what happened next.

One thing led to another. And another.
And another.

Spilt paint.

Sparking laptop.

Flaming book.

A fire swept along the table.

Quick, quick, quick.

I ripped a curtain from the window and frantically beat out the flames.

Phew. That was close.

There wasn't much damage really.

It was funny how you could fool yourself.

For about two seconds.

I was gone. I was history.

The place was a mess.

Images of a terrible future filled my head.

I wondered if the chickens would be taken for evidence. Maybe they would be locked up with me…

It was time to escape before someone grabbed me.

The house was filled with silence. No one stirred.

Then it struck me. There was no one home. All the people were gone. The whole area had been evacuated because of the floods. And I wasn't stealing. I was just taking the chickens home to roost. I was returning them to their owners.

I looked at the stuffed hens and roosters.

They were made of felt, soft leather and feathers.

Made by children, for children. Most were about

the size of a real chook. All except one.

It was huge.

Every cuddly chicken had a tag with the name of the person who had made it.

I checked out the big chicken. I already thought
I knew who it belonged to. And I wasn't wrong.

Samantha's chicken was the king of chickens.
It was a monster. It was bigger than me.

I wondered why she had made such a large chook.
Maybe it was easier for a blind person to handle
big things.

For just a second I let my mind wander. Imagine if you could breed a real chicken that size. A whole family could live off it for a month.

You could make a fortune. I made a note to mention it to Dad as a business proposition. We could grow King Sized Chickens. Or maybe breed chickens with three legs.

Private Ricky's KSC.

I pushed the thought out of my mind. This giant toy chicken was going to be a problem. How could I possibly carry it and all the other little ones over the river?

I grabbed two of the smaller chickens and pushed each of them into a bin liner. That's all I could fit in. I rose into the air with one in each hand.

Then I flew out of the room and into the front yard. Then up, higher and higher, across the river. I kept my eyes skinned for any curious creatures or people. But I was alone in the night.

I flew over the flooded paddocks until I came to firm ground on the other side.

'Down,' I said to myself. I dropped to the ground and looked around.

And saw it.

The Great Great White. A fibreglass shark abandoned in a paddock. It used to be famous in our town.

Old Fishhead Finnigan had tried to set up the Ocean World theme park years ago. But it went broke because his seaweed sandwiches didn't sell. They must have been too salty.

Anyway, the shark was all that was left.

And it was just what I needed to keep the toy chooks dry while I went back for a few more.

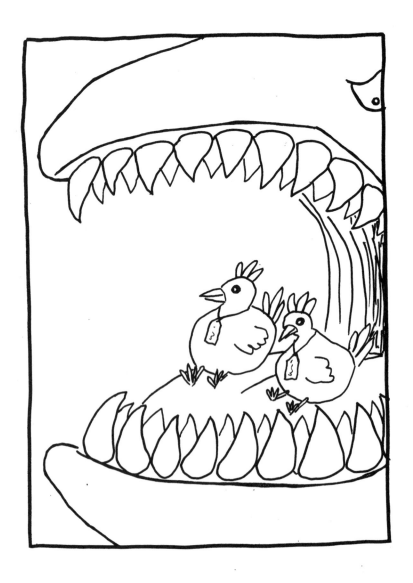

I flew into the air and returned to the Hobby Farm. I had to be quick. There were around twenty toys and I could only bring two at a time. I couldn't risk dropping them.

Back I went.

Time was passing. It was already growing light.

Back I went. Again. And again. And again.

There was only one chicken to go. Samantha's giant one.

I flew back and lifted it up with both hands. It was filled with foam beads, like a beanbag. It was heavy, but I thought that I could just manage to fly with it.

I had to be careful. Hundreds of chicken feathers had been sewn all over the outside. Samantha wouldn't like it if I tore any off or dropped the whole chook into the water.

'Up,' I said.

Up I went.

'Forward,' I said.

I flew low over the rushing river. At times
it seemed to reach up at me with watery arms.
I held onto the giant chicken with great difficulty.
It was awkward and I could feel it slipping out
of my grasp.

But in the end all the chickens were on the right
side of the river.

The sun began to throw golden shards into the sky.

Soon the whole world would be awake.

5

No Room Inside

The countryside was coming to life.
I had to be quick. I had to get twenty stuffed chickens to Samantha's house before I was seen.

There wasn't enough time for ten or eleven trips.

What could I do? Think, think, think.

Yes, yes that was it. A plan. Not a perfect plan, but the best that I could do.

I grabbed Samantha's giant chook and turned it around. There was a zip running all the way down the front. I unzipped it and threw the foam beads to the wind. They flew off like flurries of snow. In no time at all the chook was empty.

All the small chickens fitted snugly inside.

All except one. A small hen with a sad red eye.

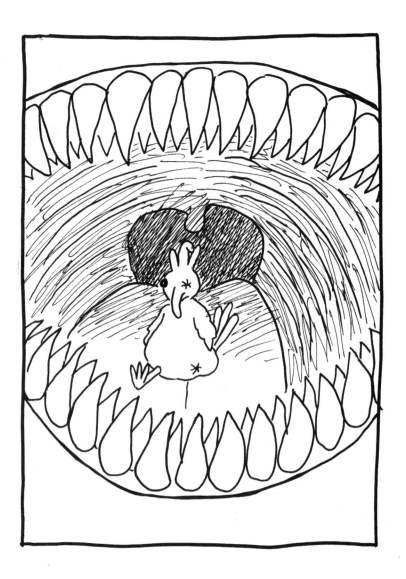

I tried as hard as I could, but I just couldn't
fit it in. Time was passing quickly.

'Sorry, Red Eye,' I said. 'But I am going to have
to leave you behind. There just isn't enough
room for you.'

I grabbed Samantha's giant chook.

I rose into the air.

This time the huge chook was even heavier than before. The small chickens were packed in tight.

I concentrated as hard as I could.

Faster and faster I flew. Over the paddocks.
Across roads and farms. And finally rooftops.
It was broad daylight, but I was nearly there.

A woman on a bike cycled far below, but
fortunately she didn't look up.

There it was. At Last. Samantha's house.

With my last remaining strength I lowered myself
and my feathery burden onto the front porch.
I quickly pulled out the stuffed toys and sat them
one by one along the house wall. Then I dropped
Samantha's empty chook skin to the ground.

The line of rescued chickens seemed to be smiling
at me. I smiled back at the toys I had saved.

But then the smile fell from my lips.

A small jab of guilt stung me like a wasp.

One chicken was not there.

One chicken had been left behind.

Red Eye.

She was still in the shark, staring out at the paddock, alone and unloved.

Later in the day all the kids would be happily winning ribbons and getting certificates. All except one kid. Probably some poor boy or girl who was having a bad, bad day.

Red Eye could belong to someone who had no friends. Maybe they were even teased. Or told that they looked like a chicken.

Maybe in the years to come they would never forget the day their chook was left alone in a rotting shark's mouth.

Their life ruined forever. All because of me.

I had to go back. I had to get Red Eye. But how? The one-eyed toy was far away, across flooded fields. The sun was up and shining down brightly.

Someone would see me flying for sure.

I had to get to Red Eye without anyone seeing me fly.

An image of the Pterodactyl flitted through my head.

Yes, yes, yes.

Just the thing.

It would be dangerous.

It would be scary.

But I was no chicken.

So I did it.

I flew inside a…

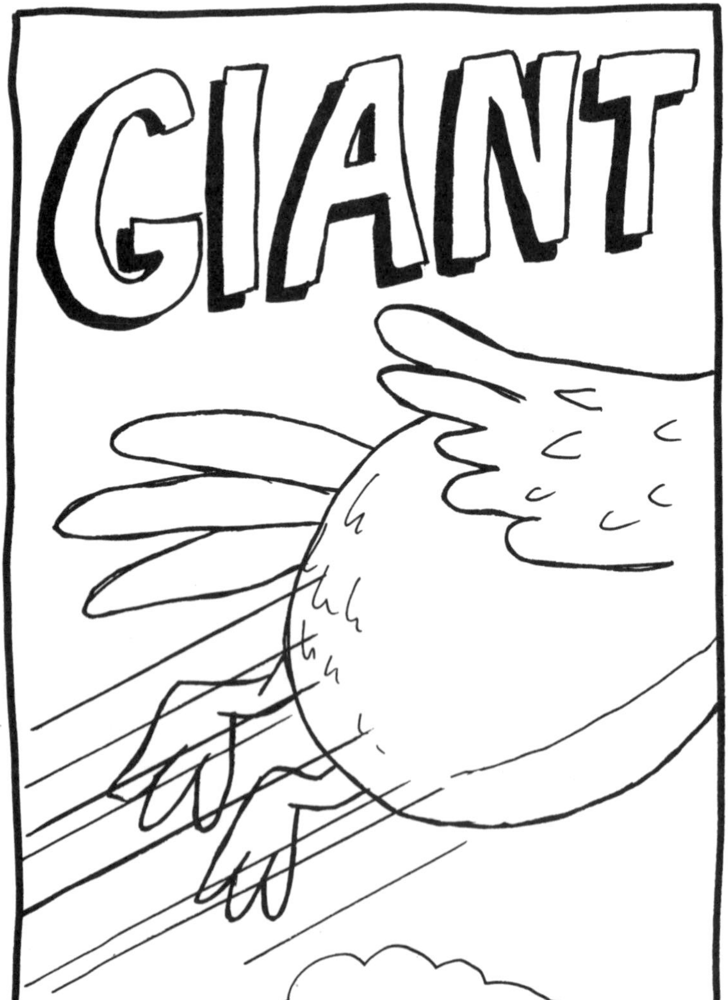
GIANT

I was safe from falling because I was inside the chicken. No one could see me.

Up, I flew. Up, up, up.

It felt fantastic.

I was a superhero.

I was…Chicken Man.

I sped through the sky. It was hard to see out of the beak but, after much swooping and twisting, I made it.

The final journey was not without problems. Two swans flying to distant fields dived on me, but I did a loop-the-loop and escaped their snapping beaks.

As I neared home I saw something unexpected.

Mandy Chow.

The girl who called me 'Chook'.

She was probably making her way to The Show.

If she looked up it wouldn't matter. I was safe inside the feathery chicken suit. I wouldn't fall to my death.

I shouldn't have done it. But I couldn't help myself.

I swooped low and hovered just over her head.

I made a loud clucking noise.

I flapped my wings.

Her eyes grew round as she saw the huge bird in the air just above her head.

'Mum, Mum, Mum,' she shouted as she fled along the path.

'Do I look like a chicken?' I squawked.

Then I flew away. I didn't want to be too cruel. Enough was enough. And there wasn't much time left before The Show started.

I landed on Samantha's porch once more.
I placed Red Eye down with the other chickens.
Then I shrugged off the big chicken skin.
It dropped to my feet like a worn-out rug.

I had done it. Every kid would have a chicken
for The Show. Except Samantha.

Her giant chicken was as flat as an old rug.
I needed something to stuff it with. Quickly.
I looked around her front yard. Nothing.

I ran home as quickly as I could. I was desperate. I needed something to put inside Samantha's chicken. I looked around my bedroom. There was only one thing I could think of that would do the trick.

'No, not that,' I said to myself. 'You can't.'

But I did.

6

Showing off

Samantha thanked me about a million times. She couldn't stop smiling. Neither could all the other kids.

She knew that I had saved the day. I was definitely a hero.

I couldn't tell her that I had flown home with the chickens. She wouldn't believe me.

So I showed off instead.

'Those chooks were heavy,' I said. 'But I managed it, no worries. I'm stronger than I look.'

The kids were so proud.

Red Eye did especially well.

Samantha's big chicken won a prize too.

Samantha was rapt.

'The judges would have given me first,' she said,
'but they told me that my chicken smelled of
pee and they had to take a couple of points off
for that.'

She gave me a big hug.

Mum was happy too. She was glad that my
old doona had been used for such a good cause.
And she bought me a new one. It was really warm.
The best you can get.

Story Two

SEEING
RED

1

Smoke

'**W**hat's the colour grey like?' asked Samantha as we walked along the track through the forest.

'Smoke is grey,' I said.

Samantha smiled. 'Yes, I know that,' she said. 'Even though I'm blind I know what colour things are. The sky is blue and leaves are green. And smoke is black or grey. But…'

She was searching for the right words.

Finally she said, 'What are colours really *like*?
How do they make you feel?'

That was a tricky question. If she couldn't
see a colour, how could she get an idea of it?

I thought hard. I wanted to please her.
She was the nicest person in the world.

'Well,' I said. 'Yellow is a happy colour.'

'What about orange?' she said.

I thought a bit more.

'Orange is the memory of something good,' I said.

I was starting to get the hang of it. I liked describing how a colour made me feel.

'So what about grey?' she asked.

I tried to explain what grey felt like.

'Grey is a bit sad,' I said. 'Not miserable. Not angry. Just a little unhappy.'

'And red?' she asked.

'Red is…'

I was going to say what I was feeling, but she beat me to it.

Samantha gave her dog, Jack, a cuddle and said, 'Red is for love.'

She loved Jack a lot. He didn't seem to notice the cuddle though. He was too busy sniffing the air.

Lucky Jack. I wished Samantha was giving me a cuddle.

But I wasn't jealous. How could I be jealous of a dog like him?

He was a great dog, was Jack. Real smart.

SOME THINGS YOU SHOULD KNOW ABOUT **JACK**.

- Has had special Guide Dog training. Stops at crossings, catches bullets with teeth, etc. (Last one a guess.)

- Kind, wise eyes.

- Kind, wise ears.

- Doesn't bite (only food).

- Very pattable. You're not supposed to pat Guide Dogs when they're working, but its hard because he's so extremely pattable.

- Slobbery. It doesn't get in the way of his Guide Dog duties though.

- Loyal. Would do anything for Samantha (within limits of his doggy abilities).

Jack was still sniffing.

'He can smell something,' I said.

Samantha nodded. 'Dogs have a fantastic sense of smell,' she said. 'So do blind people. But not as good as dogs.'

I changed the subject. I was thinking of something else.

I had two big problems.

The first one was flying. Well, flying wasn't the problem. That was a good thing. But I wanted everyone in the world to know that I could do it. I wanted to be on TV. And in the papers. I wanted to be a star at school, and not a loner.

And I wanted Samantha to believe that I could fly. I wanted her to know how I saved her life.

My memory floated back to that day.

She hadn't even known I was flying. Because she was blind.

Today I was going to prove it to her. I was going to prove that I really could fly. Even though she wouldn't let me mention it.

The second problem I had was more urgent.

I was busting.

2

Taking Pictures

There's nothing worse than needing to pee when you can't. It's agony.

Once when Dad was driving me and Mum to the beach, I was busting to go. Dad wouldn't stop the car because we were on the freeway.

Mum gave me a lecture.

'I told you to go to the toilet before we left home,' she said. 'And you didn't. So now you'll just have to wait until we get there.'

I was in the back seat of the car with a bunch of old beach toys, including a bucket and spade.

I'm not proud of what I did, but I had no choice.

Silently I filled the bucket with pee.

Oh, it was so good. What a relief.

I didn't say anything to Dad or Mum because
they would just have gone on and on about it.

I hate it when parents go on and on and never
let you forget what you did wrong.

But I had a problem. A big problem.

Dad's driving.

'Slow down on the curves,' I said. 'I'm feeling carsick.'

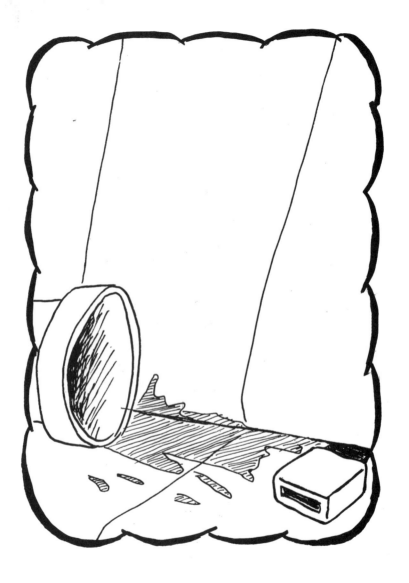

It was Dad's fault.

I did ask him to take the corners carefully.

Talk about going on and on. Even though it was about fifty years ago, Mum still mentions it every time we go to the beach. What a fuss. I mean the smell never left her car, but it wasn't that bad.

What's a bit of pee between friends?

A big fuss over nothing.

But that was long ago.

This time I was busting and I wasn't stuck in the car. I was walking through the forest with Samantha, the beautiful car-wash girl.

She was my friend. My only friend. And I didn't want to lose her. I couldn't say, 'Can we stop so I can pee?'

That would be so embarrassing.

Samantha is great fun, but she's a very refined girl. She never slurps when she eats soup. She never even makes a gurgling noise when she drinks a milkshake through a straw. That's class.

If I peed while she was nearby she might think
I was crude. Or rude.

But I was just about bursting with the effort of
holding it in. I really needed to go and I couldn't
concentrate on all this talk about what colours
felt like.

'What's white like?' she asked.

'Think of something cold,' I said.

I shouldn't have said that. Or thought it.

It made my problem even worse.

I took her hand and tried to hurry her along the winding track. With every step my agony grew worse.

The forest was hot and dry. We were miles from anywhere and there wasn't another person to be seen. Every now and then Jack would sniff the air.

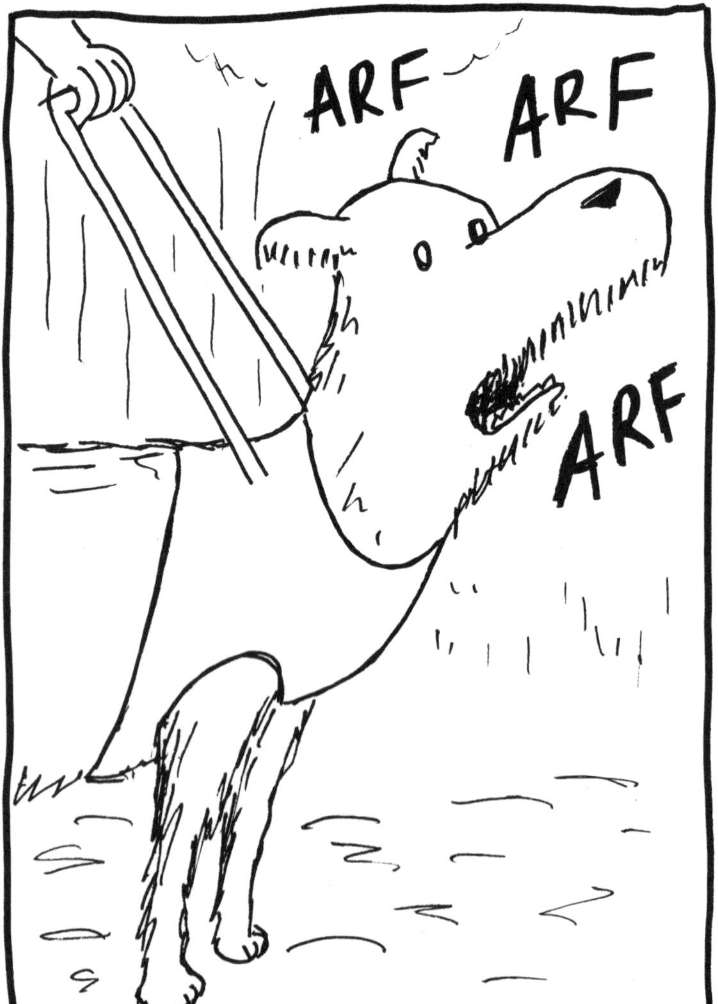
ARF
ARF
ARF

'Is he jealous?' I asked.

Samantha laughed and gave him another pat.

'He's not jealous,' she said. 'He can smell something odd.'

It was a great day. The sun was warm in a blue sky. I took out my camera. I decided to take some pictures.

'Smile,' I said.

Samantha looked straight at the camera.

Click.

It was a terrific shot.

'How did you know where to look?' I said.

'Give me the camera,' she said.

I handed it to her.

'Put my finger on the button,' she said.

'The left button is for taking a photo,' I said.
'And the right is for video.'

I put her finger on the shutter button.

Jack was sitting in the shade nearby. Samantha
pointed the camera straight at him and pressed.

Click.

It was a lovely photo. Jack was licking himself. Very tasteful. For Jack anyway. And really well-framed. Just a little bit of his tail was missing.

'Perfect,' I said. 'Amazing. Tell me the secret.'

'People who can't see develop their other senses,' she said. 'I have great hearing and a great sense of smell. I could hear Jack breathing, so I knew where to point the camera.'

I held out my hand. 'I'll take another photo of you,' I said.

Samantha didn't answer. Now it was her turn to sniff the air.

'I can smell smoke,' she said.

'Don't worry,' I said. 'It could be anything.'

But there was a word in the back of my mind. A word that I pushed down deep and tried not to think about.

'Let me take another photo,' I said.

'No,' said Samantha. She put the camera in her pocket. 'That smell of smoke worries me. Let's get going.'

'Okay,' I said. 'Let's go to the lookout tower and find out where it's coming from.'

3

Look Out

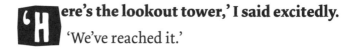

'**H**ere's the lookout tower,' I said excitedly. 'We've reached it.'

The tower stood in the middle of a clearing. Dry grass grew all around.

'What does it look like?' said Samantha.

'It's very high,' I said. 'It's made of steel so that it won't catch fire. On the top there is a hut with windows.'

'How do you get up?' said Samantha.

'It has a narrow staircase going around and around. But it's broken and most of the steps are missing. No one could get up there.'

Samantha looked worried.

'There's a sign,' I said.

'What does it say?' she asked.

'It's just rubbish,' I said. 'It doesn't mean anything.'

I stared and stared at it.

The sign reminded me of one of those puzzles teachers make you do after you have finished reading a story. You have to put in the missing letters.

Boring.

But gradually it became clear.

'Ah, ha, I get it,' I said. 'It's dangerous. We can't go up there.'

I walked on to find a spot to sit down.

'There might be snakes in the long grass,' said Samantha. 'I don't want Jack to get bitten. Don't go through any grass.'

We sat down on some rocks and unpacked our picnic. There was no view from where we sat. We were surrounded by trees. The tower reached up above them.

We were alone on a big hill.

Suddenly Jack lifted his nose and sniffed again. He gave a little whine. Samantha stood and walked straight over to him. She gave him a pat. Then she sniffed the air too.

'More smoke,' she said. 'Can't you smell it?'

I didn't have time to answer.

I just had to pee or I would do it in my pants.

'I'll be back in a sec,' I yelled.

I ran down the track.

Oh what a relief. Finally my misery was over.

Why was I standing behind a tree? Samantha couldn't see what I was doing.

It was strange, but I just couldn't have done it in front of her. Even if she couldn't see me. It wouldn't have been right.

When I got back to the clearing, Samantha looked up.

She said, 'Does that feel better?'

My face started to burn. How did she know? Oh, no, no, no. She had a great sense of smell. She must have smelled the pee.

How embarrassing.

'Sorry,' I said. 'I had to go.'

She laughed. 'It's okay,' she said. 'I knew what you were doing.'

Of course. How stupid of me. She had a great sense of hearing too.

It was still embarrassing though.

As we sat on the rocks my mind returned to flying.
Now was the chance to prove I could do it.

I could fly in front of her safely because she
wouldn't see me.

But what was the use of that?

There must be some way to prove to her that
I could fly. She could hear and smell just about
anything.

An idea crept into my mind.

Yes. That was it. There was a way to use her special talents to let her know that I was flying.

But what about Jack? If a dog saw me flying, I would drop like a stone.

'Would you like me to move Jack into the shade?' I said. 'It's getting hot.'

'Thanks, Ricky. That's very kind of you,' she said.

I led Jack to a shady spot where he was out of the sun.

He wouldn't be able to see us. Perfect.

Samantha stared at the bushes. She knew where Jack was. She could hear him panting.

I willed myself to rise.

'Hi, Samantha,' I said.

'What are you doing?' she said.

'I'm flying,' I said. 'Up here. Can't you tell?'

'Don't start that silly nonsense again, Ricky,'
she said.

'I'm not,' I said. 'I'll go higher. Listen to where my
voice is coming from.'

'Up,' I said to myself.

I rose a couple more metres and called out Samantha's name.

She yelled back.

'I know you're faking.'

'I'm not,' I said.

She was getting angry.

'It's not fair of you to try to trick me just because I can't see. No one else believes you can fly. No one has seen you fly, because you can't. It's impossible.'

I sighed. 'I've told you, Samantha. If anyone sees me fly I will fall to the ground and die.'

She clapped her hands over her ears.

'Stop it,' she yelled. 'Don't be mean. Stop lying. I can't be friends with a liar.'

I fell silent. The only thing worse than not flying would be losing Samantha. I couldn't bear the thought of not having her for a friend.

I knew I had hurt her feelings. She thought I was trying to take advantage of her blindness. But I wasn't a liar. I was telling the truth.

I called out again. 'Up here,' I yelled.

She turned her head and listened. She was following my voice. She was looking in my direction. Exactly where I was hovering. But, of course, she couldn't see me.

'It's a trick,' she said. 'You're not flying. There are plenty of ways you can get up high.'

I knew she was right. I could think of a few myself.

I rose higher and higher.

I was almost up to the top of the trees.

'Here,' I yelled.

Surely she would realise what I was doing.
Surely she would know that my voice was coming out of the sky.

I went higher, still calling out Samantha's name.

I looked down. She was shouting at me.

I could only just hear her.

'Ricky,' she yelled. 'There is no time for this. I can smell smoke. So can Jack. He's whimpering. There is a fire somewhere. We have to get out of here.'

My heart raced. This was serious. I rose higher. I was level with the top of the tower. Now I could see over the trees. Out over the valley. And down to the bottom of the mountain.

Clouds of grey smoke swirled and boiled.

Flames licked at the sky.

Red sparks swirled like crazy bees.

I felt the wind blowing.

Towards us.

The word I had pushed down inside me leapt
out of my mouth.

Smoke and flames were coming our way.

Fast.

4

Trapped

Grey smoke drifted through the treetops. I descended as quickly as I could and landed with a thump next to Samantha.

'We have to get out of here,' I said. 'Quick.'

I stared up at the small lookout hut on the top of the tower.

It had been built as a place to spot bushfires in the old days, before satellites. It would be safe up there.

'Where's Jack?' said Samantha. Her voice was shaking.

She called out and we heard him bark in reply.

The air was hot and sparks were swirling high above. A mob of kangaroos burst out of the forest and bounded down the slope. They looked like grey rocks tumbling into the forest below.

Patches of long grass caught fire around the tower. If we didn't hurry we would be cut off from the tower. But even if we reached it, how could we get up? The stairs were broken.

We could hear flames roaring as the bushfire raced up the mountain. I had to do something. Fast.

The grass was burning furiously. There was no way we could cross it. I had to get Samantha to safety.

'I'm going to fly you over the flames,' I yelled. 'Trust me.'

'Don't be stupid,' she shouted.

I would never convince her that I could fly. She was backing away from me.

I decided to lie to her. It was the only thing I could do.

'Okay,' I said. 'I'm going to carry you. I will take you through the flames in my arms.'

'Take Jack first,' she yelled.

'No,' I said. 'I'm taking you first.'

I remembered the last time I'd flown with her. She was heavy. It was all I could do to lift her a few metres into the air. I couldn't take her and Jack together. I would never get off the ground.

She shook her head. Jack barked loudly from behind the bushes.

I grabbed her arm, but she shook me off.

'Jack, Jack, Jack,' she yelled.

The flames crackled and roared. In front of us the grass blazed and the flames licked at the steel legs of the tower. We were surrounded by fire.

Samantha wouldn't go without Jack. It was no use. I had to take him first.

I lifted off the ground and flew across the rocks towards the bushes where Jack was tied up.

I looked down at him. And he looked up at…

'Oh, no, no, no.'

ARF ARF ARF ARF ARF
ARF
ARF
ARF
ARF
ARF
ARF ARF
ARF
ARF
ARF ARF ARF
ARF ARF

Wham. I crashed to the ground. I managed
to get up and stagger over to Jack.

I couldn't fly while he was looking at me.
This had happened to me before. I remembered
the dog I had saved at school. The one that fell
down the hole.

I knew what I had to do.

I quickly whipped off my T-shirt.

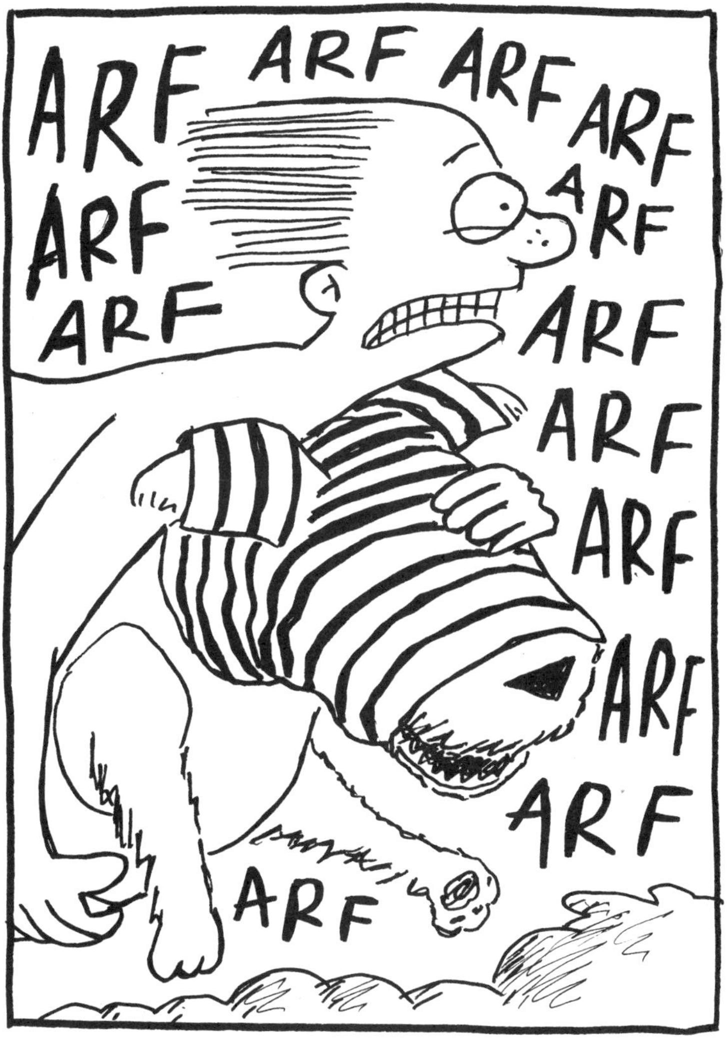
ARF
ARF
ARF
ARF
ARF
ARF
ARF
ARF
ARF
ARF
ARF
ARF
ARF
ARF

Now I could fly without being seen. I just hoped that all the kangaroos had gone.

Jack barked and wriggled. He didn't like having the T-shirt over his head. Even though he couldn't see, he could sense that he was up in the air.

'Quiet, boy,' I said. 'It's okay. I've got you.'

Jack struggled and barked even more loudly, but I held him firmly. I gave it everything I had and we soared through the air. Up above the smoke. Up above Samantha. Higher and higher.

The smoke and heat made me choke. I was tempted to drop Jack and go back for Samantha. But I knew it would be a bad idea.

Samantha would never forgive me.

Far below I could see her face turned up towards us. She could hear Jack barking.

I had never flown so quickly before.

I landed on top of the lookout tower with a bump and pushed open the hut door. I shoved Jack inside and shut him in.

As I leapt off the tower I could still hear him barking loudly behind me.

5

Happy Landing

n a moment I was by Samantha's side.

'Jack?' she yelled.

'He's safe,' I said. 'On top of the tower.'

I put one arm under her knees and the other around her waist. I lifted her gently.

Samantha clung onto my neck and I flew with her in my arms. She was heavy. Flying with a weight was even harder than carrying something on the ground.

My muscles ached. My brain strained. Sweat mixed with the smoke and ran into my eyes. It stung and made it difficult to see.

Beneath us the flames reached up like fiery hands.

Up, up, up. We rose past the first level of the tower. And the second. From high above came the sound of barking.

I counted the platforms as we passed. I wanted to stop and land on one of them, but I knew that Samantha would never stay put without Jack.

One flight of stairs. Another. Then another. We were almost there.

'Jack, Jack, Jack,' screamed Samantha.

A cold fear swept through my aching limbs. If Jack escaped from the hut and looked down …

The higher we flew, the heavier Samantha seemed. I strained and sweated. I reached the bottom of the top platform. Just a metre more.

We made it.

Yes, yes, yes. I fell onto the landing with my precious bundle. Jack burst out of the door and bounded into Samantha's open arms.

For just a second I was jealous.

In half an hour the fire had passed and disappeared down the hill.

After a while we heard a motor.

It was getting closer.

We'd been found.

Between me and Dad we managed to fly Jack and Samantha down to the ground. She was very grateful and thanked me about a thousand times for carrying her to safety.

Dad winked at me and tapped his nose. I knew he didn't want her to know the truth. He didn't want anyone to know that we could fly.

He drove Samantha through the blackened forest on the quad bike, with Jack running alongside. Then he came back for me. I couldn't risk flying home. There were firemen and fire trucks everywhere.

I didn't see Samantha for a week. I didn't want to.

I couldn't face up to pretending that I had carried her to safety. I wanted to tell her that I had flown with her. But she would just get angry.

It was a boring week. Even comics seemed less exciting than they'd used to.

Then, Samantha suddenly arrived at our door with Jack. She was excited.

'Put this in your computer,' she said.

I did what she said. And there I was.

Flying.

I couldn't believe it. I was on the screen. Flying through the smoke. Carrying Jack. There he was struggling and barking. I saw myself vanish into a cloud of smoke and reappear above it.

I saw myself look down with smoke and sweat stinging my eyes. Sparks and burning leaves swirled around me.

Finally I landed on the platform.

Jack and I disappeared into the lookout hut and the credits came up.

'You pointed my camera at Jack barking,' I said
 excitedly.

'Yes. And your camera was still in my backpack
when I got home. Dad helped me make a short
film. He thinks it's a digital trick, but I know
it's true.'

'We can put it on the internet. And everyone will
know I can fly. I'll be…'

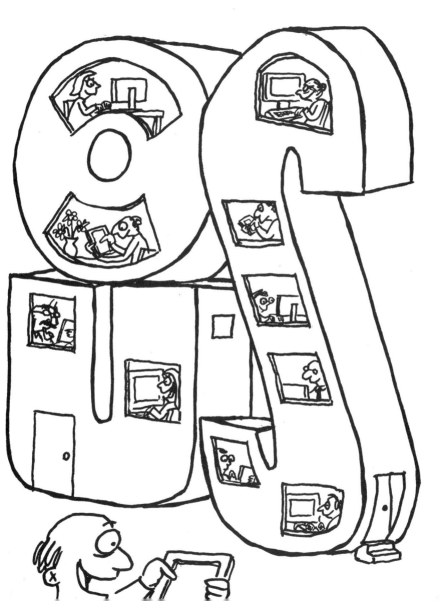

'Yes,' said Samantha. 'People will think it's special effects. But they'll love it. You'll be famous. For acting.'

'So nothing will change,' I said. 'No one will believe I can fly. Only Mum and Dad.'

'And me,' said Samantha. 'I believe you can fly.'

I thought about it for just a second. That was all I needed. Samantha believed I could fly. It was all that was important. Next to that, fame was nothing.

'How does that make you feel, Ricky?' said Samantha.

This time I didn't have to think.

'Yellow,' I said. 'It makes me feel yellow. What about you?'

'Yes, yellow,' she answered. She touched my hand.

'And a bit of red, too.'

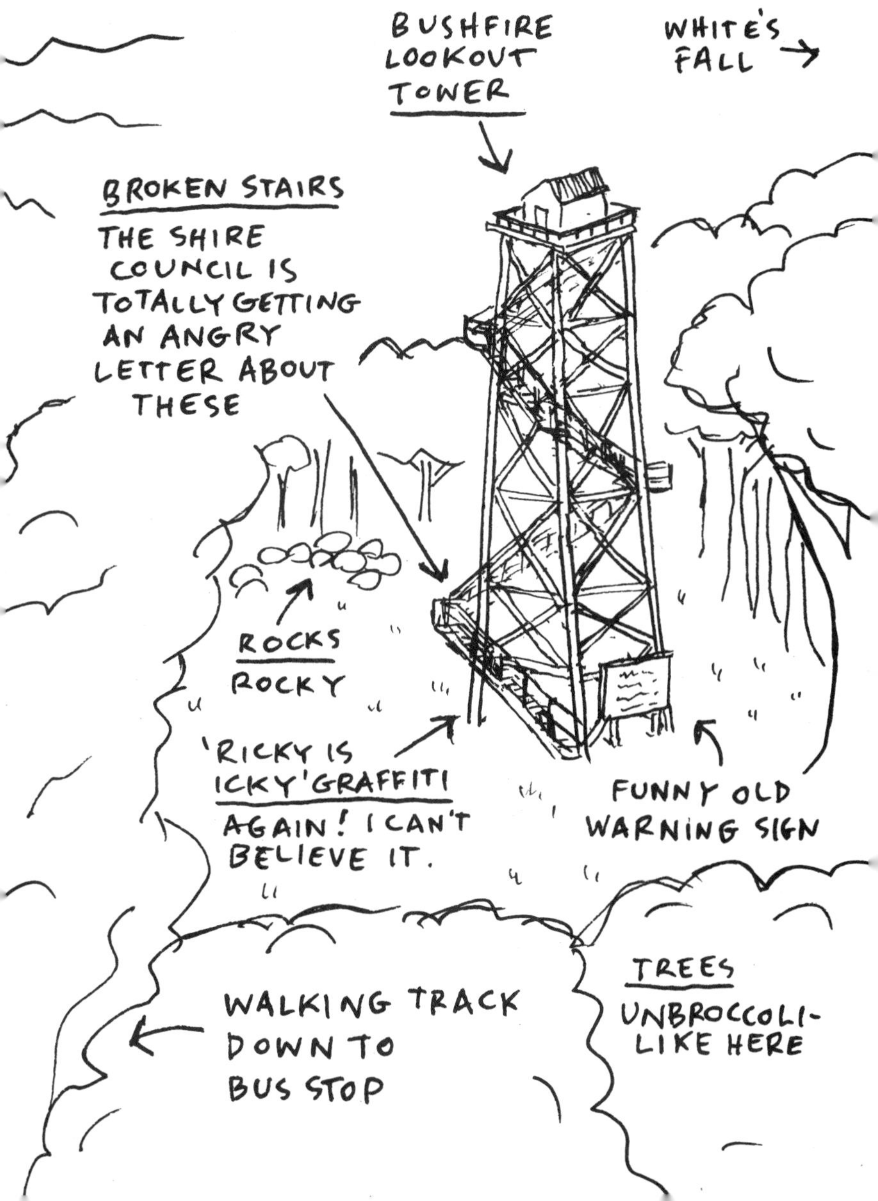
BUSHFIRE LOOKOUT TOWER
WHITE'S FALL →
BROKEN STAIRS
THE SHIRE COUNCIL IS TOTALLY GETTING AN ANGRY LETTER ABOUT THESE
ROCKS
ROCKY
'RICKY IS ICKY' GRAFFITI
AGAIN! I CAN'T BELIEVE IT.
FUNNY OLD WARNING SIGN
TREES
UNBROCCOLI-LIKE HERE
WALKING TRACK DOWN TO BUS STOP

COLLECT THE SET